Written by

Heather Avis

EVERYONE
BELONGS

Illustrated by

Sarah Mensinga

WATERBROOK

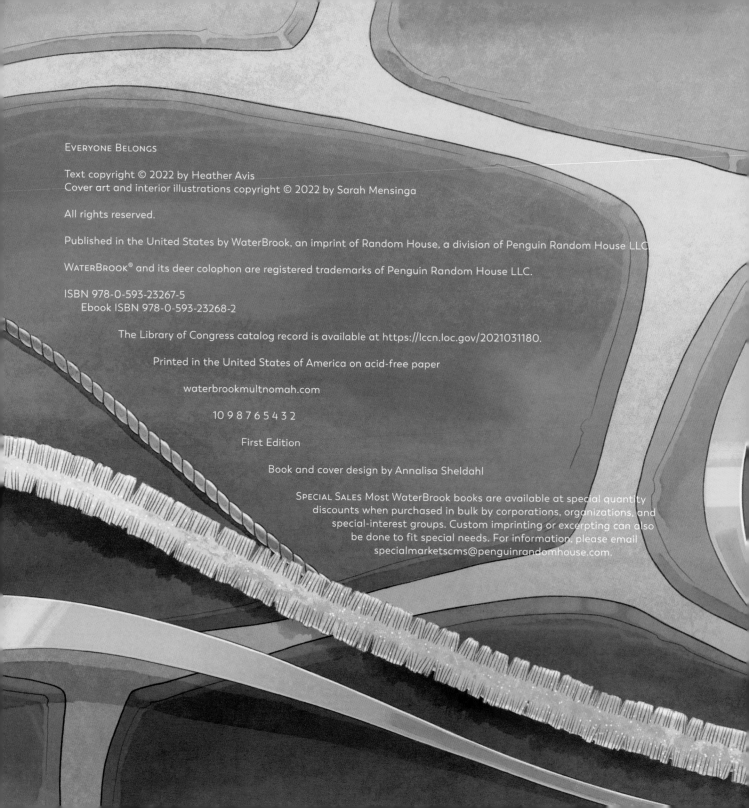

Published in the United States by WaterBrook, an imprint of Random House, a division of Penguin Random House LLC.

WaterBrook® and its deer colophon are registered trademarks of Penguin Random House LLC.

ISBN 978-0-593-23267-5
   Ebook ISBN 978-0-593-23268-2

The Library of Congress catalog record is available at https://lccn.loc.gov/2021031180.

Printed in the United States of America on acid-free paper

waterbrookmultnomah.com

10 9 8 7 6 5 4 3 2

First Edition

Book and cover design by Annalisa Sheldahl

Special Sales Most WaterBrook books are available at special quantity
discounts when purchased in bulk by corporations, organizations, and
special-interest groups. Custom imprinting or excerpting can also
be done to fit special needs. For information, please email
specialmarketscms@penguinrandomhouse.com.

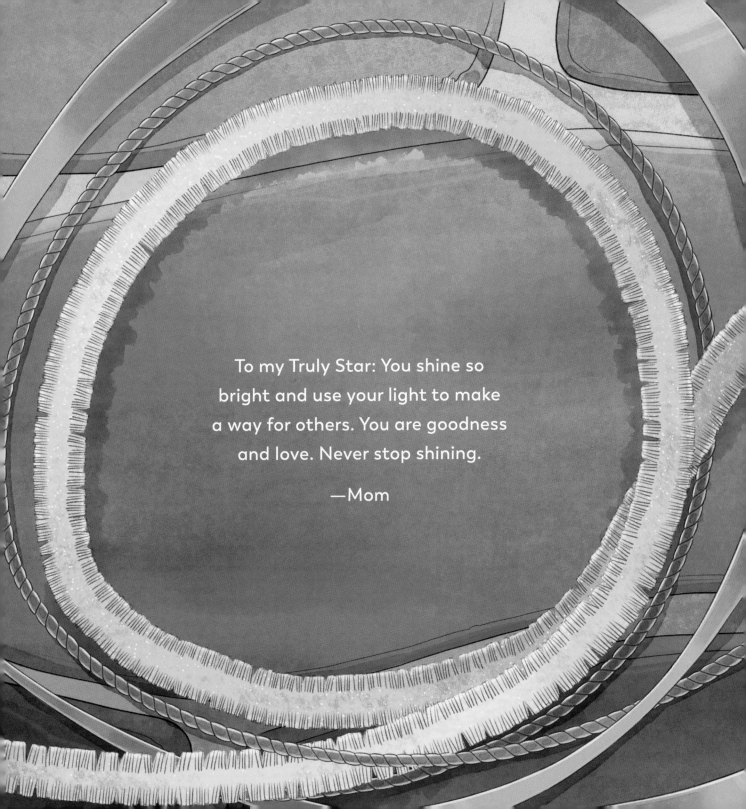

To my Truly Star: You shine so
bright and use your light to make
a way for others. You are goodness
and love. Never stop shining.

—Mom

Have I got a story to share with you,
one about sisters named Macy and Tru.
It's a tale of two girls and one fabulous show,
and you are invited. So come on, let's go!

Macy's the older sister of the two.
She leads by example, as the eldest will do.
She shows up bravely, exactly as she is,
an inspiration to all, a magnificent kid!

Though Tru is taller, she's the younger one.
She's bold and confident, getting stuff done.
Tru loves meeting new people, making a pal.
She's the world-changing type, a powerful gal.

Macy and Tru are unalike, as you see,
but they know that Different is a great thing to be!
The sisters both wanted to glitter and glow
and together declared, "We will shine in a show!"

The girls made their way to the stage in the park.
There was much to be done, tasks on which to embark.
With their arms full of tutus, capes, wigs, and a mic,
they soon caught the eye of a kid on his bike.

The boy, named Lamar, walked close to the stage,
and the singing sisters looked up from their page.
"Oh, hi, I'm Macy; my sister is Tru.
Have we got the most perfect part just for you!"

Lamar's eyes looked delighted, but then they turned sad,
and he wrote something on an electric notepad:
"Singing is not something I do, you see.
I use this device—is there still room for me?"

Tru tossed him a ribbon, so shiny and thick.
"Exactly who you are is exactly who we pick.
We know everyone's Different; no two are the same.
You belong in our show!" the sisters exclaimed.

Lamar jumped on the stage, ribbon high in the air.
Then Nova appeared, showing style and flair.
She wore fancy sunglasses and held a white cane.
"What's going on here?" she asked bold and plain.

"We're doing a show. Want to help us?" asked Tru.

"But I can't see the stage. I'll need help from you two."

"Of course! Take our hands," the sisters announced.

"You still have a role: you can sing, twirl, or bounce."

Macy gave her a tutu. "This should do the trick!
Exactly who you are is exactly who we pick.
We know everyone's Different; no two are the same.
You belong in our show!" the sisters exclaimed.

Now all the commotion was drawing a crowd.
So many kids wondered if they were allowed
to join in the show and be part of this thing.
What if someone felt shy or did not like to sing?

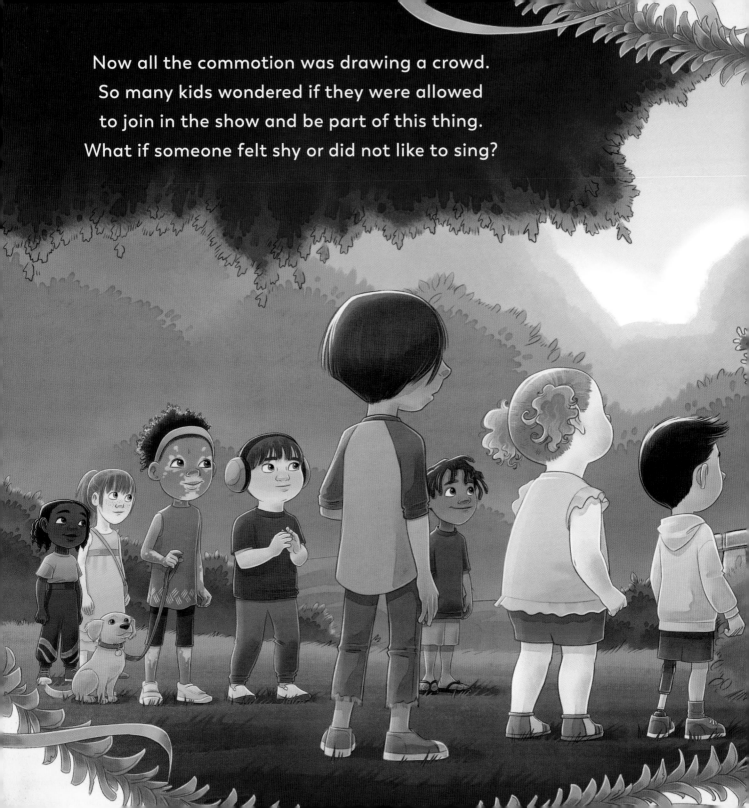

As more people gathered, Tru looked at each face.
"We're so happy you're here. You're in the right place.
We need all of you friends to help with this show!
Everyone belongs here, I hope that you know."

Macy stood by her sister and nodded her head.
Excitement was growing and starting to spread.
Yet some kids felt anxious, unsure where to go.
Many wondered out loud, "How can I help the show?"

"You can sing, you can shout, you can whistle or snap.
You can dance, you can twirl, you can hum, you can flap.
Don't like the attention? Then come on backstage.
There are plenty of ways for you to engage."

The growing crowd of kids leaped up to help out.
With glitter and tulle, they all bustled about.
If each played their part, doing what they did best,
this show would undoubtedly be a success!

While Tru stayed quite busy with costumes and glue,
pointing this way and that, telling kids what to do,
Macy spotted a boy in a power wheelchair.
She said to her sis, "What's his name, over there?"

Tru knew him from school. "Oh, his name is Shepp."
Then she noticed: no ramp, only step after step.
While the show could go on without Shepp and his chair,
she knew leaving out others is not kind and not fair.

Tru looked at the stage and her beautiful set.
Her friend turned his chair, eyes filled with regret.
Tru knew what it felt like when she was left out.
We all want to belong, she knew without doubt.

But cardboard and tutus and glitter and glue
could not build a ramp. This just would not do!
The group became quiet; no one made a sound.
"The space is the problem, not how he gets around."

"Hey, Shepp!" Tru called out. "Come over here, quick!
Exactly who you are is exactly who we pick.
We know you belong in this show we are showing,
so we'll move it to you. Everyone, let's get going!"

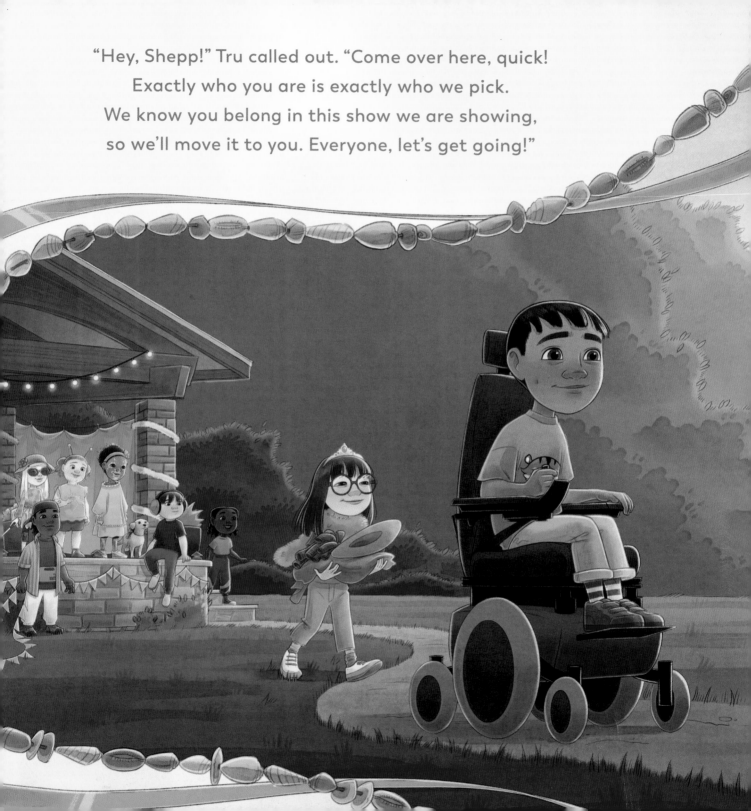

The kids in the show gathered up all their props:
all the costumes and ribbons, the tutus and tops.
They filled cardboard boxes with glitter and tape,
and they ran up to Shepp, a new plan taking shape.

Macy, Tru, and the crew then started to swarm,
creating a new stage where all could perform.
Shepp watched the kids working. No two were alike.
Then he whispered "Wow!" as Tru gave him the mic.

Shepp moved center stage, knowing just what to do.
"Get in your places! It's time!" shouted Tru.
"You are spectacular, just as you are.
This is your show, and you are a star!"

So there you have it, two girls and a show,
providing a way for each kid to glow.
An invitation for you to sing out your song
as you make a space where everyone can belong.

Heather Avis
Author

Heather Avis is the author of the *New York Times* bestseller *Different—A Great Thing to Be!* as well as *The Lucky Few* and *Scoot Over and Make Some Room*. Heather is also cohost of *The Lucky Few* podcast and the founder and chief visionary officer at The Lucky Few, a social awareness brand that focuses on shifting the Down syndrome narrative. She lives in Southern California with her husband, Josh, and their three kids, Macy, Truly, and August.

Sarah Mensinga
Illustrator

Sarah Mensinga has illustrated several books, including *Different: A Great Thing to Be!*, the Trillium Sisters series, and *Flipping Forward Twisting Backward*. She also writes fantasy novels and has worked on animated films such as *The Ant Bully* and *Escape from Planet Earth*. Born in Canada, Sarah lives in Texas with her family and is currently writing and illustrating a graphic novel. Find more of her work at sarahmensinga.com.